Mar[...] be
7-28-07

I love you with
all my heart.
You are so beautiful.
Gramma

We thought
you were going to
be a boy but you
came out our beautiful
Maggie.
Love
Gramma
&
Grandpa

I Loved You Before You Were Born

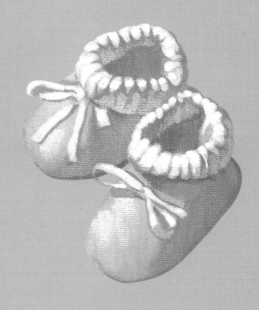

by Anne Bowen
illustrated by Greg Shed

HarperCollinsPublishers

Even before you were born,

I was your grandma

and I loved you.

I waited for you to be born,

and while I waited,

I thought about you,

dreamed about you,

wondered about you.

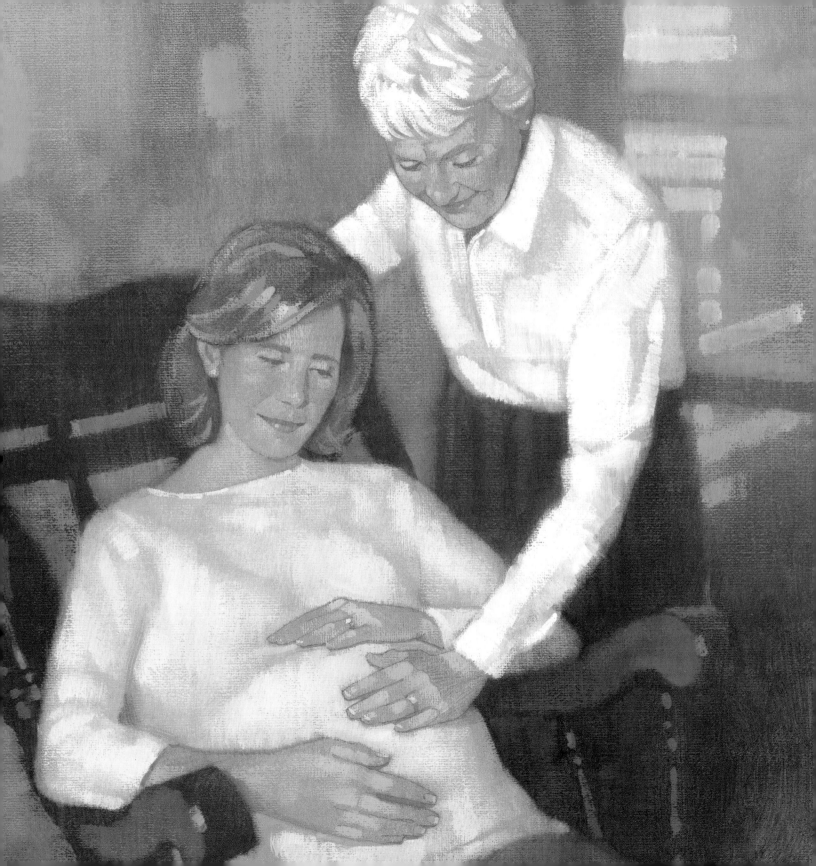

Your mommy's tummy was big and round.

Sometimes she would say to me,

"Put your hand right here."

I could feel you kicking,

just like your daddy used to kick inside my tummy.

And I wondered how much you would weigh,

and how long you would be from head to toe.

Even before you were born,

I could picture your mommy's smile

as she held you for the very first time,

and I could hear your daddy ask,

"Do you think the baby has my chin?"

I imagined your soft sighs and sweet smells

and your tiny toes lined up

like pink pearls on a necklace.

I could see your hands spread out,

like little starfish,

reaching for sunbeams

that danced on the walls of your room.

Even before you were born,

I imagined your first wide smile,

a half-moon smile,

reflected on your mommy's and daddy's faces.

I made a soft flannel blanket just for you.

And I wondered if you would carry it everywhere,

just like your daddy carried his.

I thought about reading you bedtime stories.

Dream stories.

Close-your-eyes stories.

And singing you lullabies

while your eyelids grew heavy with sleep.

I imagined holding you close,

rocking you,

watching you make faces as you dreamed.

Even before you were born,

I could see you waking up

from your afternoon nap,

tiny wrinkles of sleep

brushed across your velvet cheeks.

I saw your eyes,

round with surprise

as you rolled over by yourself

for the very first time.

I imagined you crawling

across your mommy's blue-flowered quilt,

ribbons of autumn sunlight

weaving through your hair.

Even before you were born,

I saw your daddy holding you up

to the soft glow of holiday lights

while I wrapped presents just for you.

I could picture your first birthday party,

and I saw you eating birthday cake,

pink and yellow frosting

finger painted across your face.

I imagined all these things about you,

until one day your daddy called

and said, "It's time."

Your grandpa and I rushed to join everyone

waiting just for you.

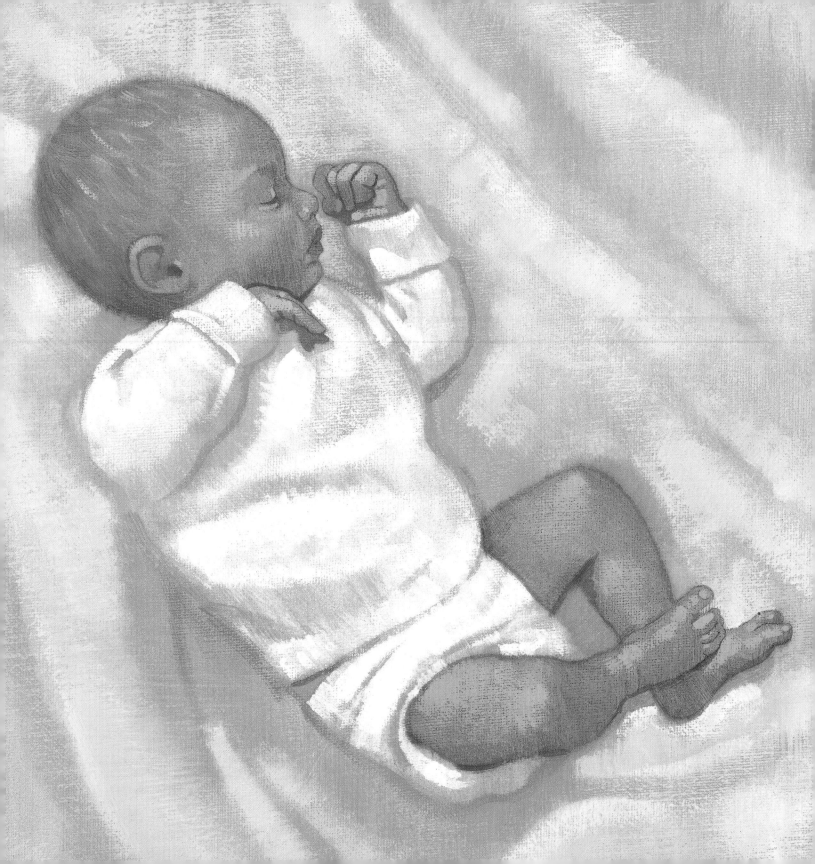

We waited for your daddy to tell us all about you:

how much you weighed,

how long you were from head to toe,

how your tiny toes lined up

like pink pearls on a necklace.

I saw your mommy smiling

as she held you for the very first time.

And I heard your daddy ask,

"Do you think the baby has my chin?"

When it was my turn,

I held you close and rocked you

and whispered,

"I am your grandma and I love you."

I loved you even before you were born.

For Addison Brooke, I loved you before you were born,
and for Peggy, who opened doors.
—A.B.

For Polly G.
—G.S.

I want to thank the women in my writing group, Susan, Becky, Kim, and Alison, for all their creative support, patience, and amazing sense of humor during the many revisions of *I Loved You Before You Were Born*.   —A.B.

I Loved You Before You Were Born   Text copyright © 2001 Anne Bowen   Illustrations copyright © 2001 by Greg Shed
Manufactured in China by South China Printing Company Ltd. All rights reserved. www.harperchildrens.com

Typography by Matt Adamec ❖